PRESENTED BY

The Zorka Mitchell
Children's Book Fund

Lunchroom Lizard

Daniel Kirk

G. P. Putnam's Sons • New York

Published simultaneously in Canada. Manufactured in China by South China Printing Co. Ltd.
Designed by Marikka Tamura. Text set in AdLib. The art was done in oil on paper.
Library of Congress Cataloging-in-Publication Data
Kirk, Daniel. Lunchroom lizard / Daniel Kirk. p. cm. Summary: Gil the gecko escapes from his
tank and wanders through the school lunchroom, where plenty of drama is unfolding.
[1. Geckos—Fiction. 2. School lunchrooms, cafeterias, etc.—Fiction. 3. Schools—Fiction.
4. Stories in rhyme.] I. Title. PZ8.3.K6553Lu 2004 [E]—dc22 2003017475
ISBN 0-399-24178-7
1 3 5 7 9 10 8 6 4 2
First Impression

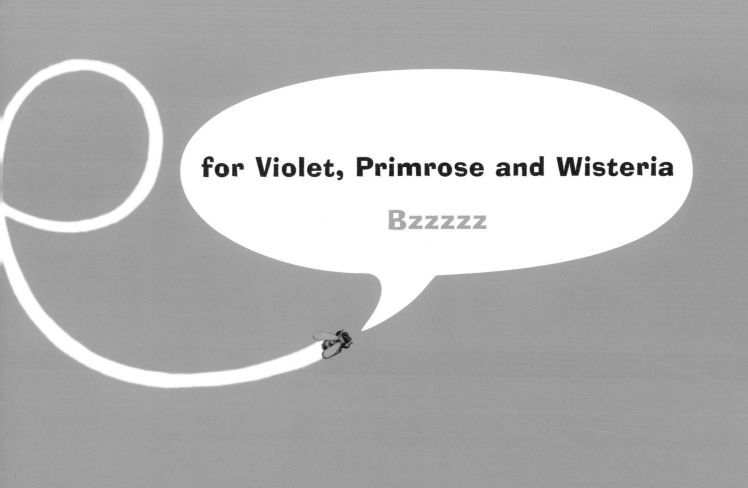

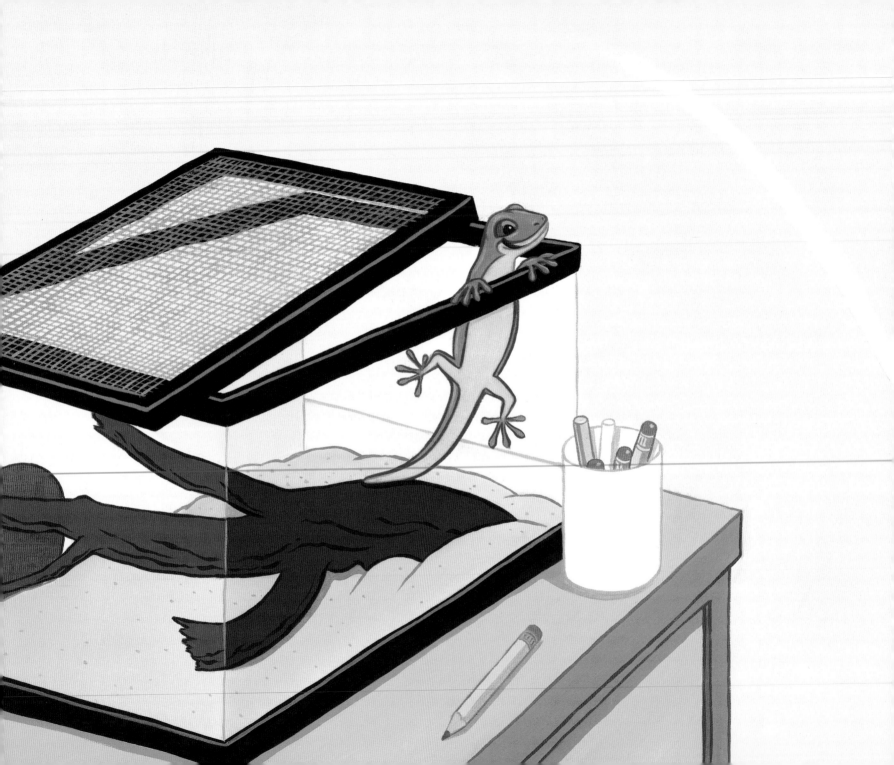

Bzzzzz!
A big, black, juicy fly
is noticed by the beady eye
of Gil the gecko, in his tank.

He's still as stone. His face is blank.
But then he leaps and bumps his snout.
The lid pops off. Surprise! He's out!

No one sees the lizard crawl.

He scurries quickly down the hall.

The fly thinks, Bzzzzz! What's that sweet smell?
and lights atop the lunchroom bell.

The bell goes off. The fly takes flight,
and Gil the gecko drops from sight.

The clock says
it is 12:01.
But where is Gil?

Kids, walk, don't run!

The clock says it is
12:06.

But where is Gil?

The clock says it is
12:15.
But where is Gil?

Has anyone seen?

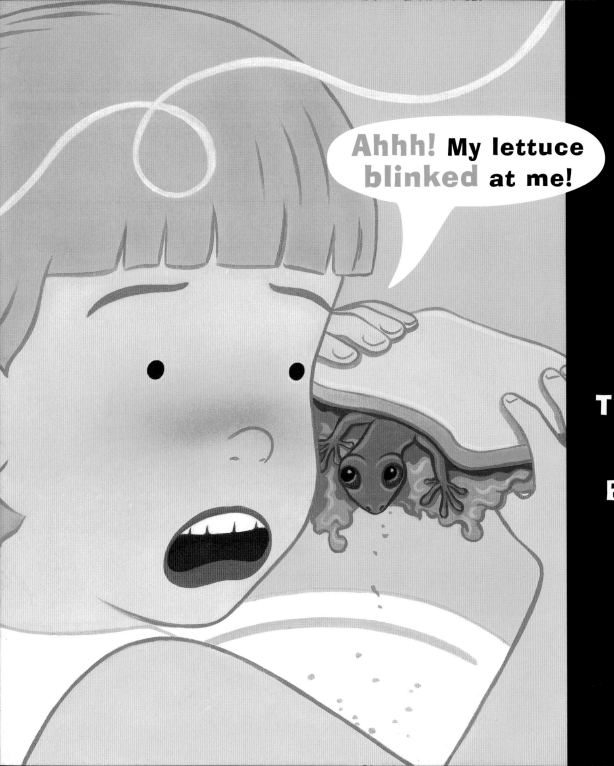

The clock says it's 12:26.
But where is Gil?

He's in a fix!

The clock says
it's 12:32.
Gil's in his tank.
He's feeling blue,
just sitting like
he always does.
The lunch that
got away goes . . .

Bzzzzz!